Starship Rescue

by

Theresa Breslin

Illustrated by Harriet Buckley

You do not need to read this page –
just get on with the book!

First published in 2005 in Great Britain by
Barrington Stoke Ltd
18 Walker Street, Edinburgh, EH3 7LP

www.barringtonstoke.co.uk

Reprinted 2008

This edition based on *Starship Rescue*, published by
Barrington Stoke in 1999

ISBN: 978-1-84299-326-2

Printed in Great Britain by Bell & Bain Ltd

Meet The Author – Theresa Breslin

What is your favourite animal?
A small elephant with green fur
What is your favourite boy's name?
Tom
What is your favourite girl's name?
Scheherazade, the Arabian princess, Teller of Tales
What is your favourite food?
Porridge and soup – but NOT together!
What is your favourite music?
Bob Dylan
What is your favourite hobby?
Reading

Meet The Illustrator – Harriet Buckley

What is your favourite animal?
A cat
What is your favourite boy's name?
Ernest
What is your favourite girl's name?
Emily
What is your favourite food?
Spinach
What is your favourite music?
"There She Goes" by The Las
What is your favourite hobby?
Playing the harmonica

This one is for Gary

Contents

Chapter 1
Outside the Fortress

10 seconds ... Just 10 seconds.

That was all the time Marc was going to have. Con, their leader, had made that very clear. The spy, Alex, had sent them a message. Tonight the Keepers of the Fortress would change the patrol on the main gate just before the planet's two suns set. It would be safe to cross the wall beside the gate then. But only for 10 seconds.

"10 seconds," Con said again. "That is how long the killer electric beam will be switched off. It is to let the guards out and in. A red light will come on. They will be given 10 seconds to change over, and then the electric beam will be turned back on again."

He gazed deep into Marc's eyes.

"They tell me that you can run fast, Marc. Let's hope that you can."

Marc listened with great care as Con told him what he had to do. He was wearing an anti-gravity belt. This would lift him up and over the wall in a few seconds. Then Marc would take the message capsule to Con who would be waiting for him in the Main Square.

"You've looked at the map?" Con asked him. "You know the way?"

Marc nodded. He knew exactly what he had to do and that it was full of danger.

Then Con, their leader, turned to the rest of the Outsiders around him, deep in the caves beside the Merkonium mines.

"Our time has come," he said. "For too long Jared and the Keepers have kept us on the Outside as slaves in the mines. Tomorrow night the Starship from our home planet Earth will pass close to our world, as it does every 20 years. The message capsule which Marc will bring into the Fortress will send out an SOS to them."

"If only they took the time to beam down on us as they passed," said one of the Outsiders. "Then they would see how we are made to slave in the Merkonium mines, while the Keepers and the Chosen Ones have a fine life inside the Fortress."

"Yes," called another. "It's time they knew how Jared, the evil Keeper, has destroyed this planet which was once so beautiful."

Con held up his hand for silence.

"It will all end soon," said Con. "Tomorrow morning I will get into the Fortress with my pass. As you all know, they let a few of us go in and out of the Fortress to buy and sell. But we have to be screened in the X-Ray booth before we can enter. The message capsule would be found if I took it in with me."

The Outsiders nodded as Con spoke.

"We have to make sure that the capsule gets to the Radio Control Station in the Fortress," said Con. Marc will carry it across the wall to me. Then we will go to the Radio Control Station, place it in the transmitter, and send out our SOS ..."

****

The Outsiders' meeting had taken place that morning. Now Marc was hidden in the bushes outside the walls of the Fortress. He looked at his watch. Five more minutes to wait. He was quite far from the wall. Could he get there in time?

He knew why he had been chosen. He was small, so he could hide in the bushes, and light so the anti-gravity belt would lift him over the wall.

He had been hiding in the bushes all day, and now it was almost time. The planet's two suns were low in the sky. In one minute the Keepers would turn off the electric beam. The red light would come on. This would last just 10 seconds to let the old patrol guards get into the Fortress and the new guards to get out.

Marc counted the seconds on his watch.

14 ... 13 ... 12 ... Marc got ready to go.

11 ...

His heart gave a jump. The red warning light had gone on at the gate.

It was time to run.

Chapter 2
Freedom Run

10!

NOW!

Marc ran towards the wall. As he ran, he counted softly.

9 ... 8 ... 7 ... 6.

Marc got to the high wall of the Fortress. He must turn on his anti-gravity belt.

His fingers slipped on the button.

"Oh no!" he said.

Marc got his finger back on the button and pressed it. He shot upwards.

"4 ... 3 ..." He counted. The wall went on and on. "2 ..."

He was at the top. Marc pressed a second button and shot forwards. He was over the top of the wall. No time for a careful landing. He crashed to the ground on the other side of the wall.

He got up as fast as he could and limped towards some thick bushes. As he crept in among them Marc felt for the message capsule inside his pocket. It was safe!

Then he heard someone call, "This way!"

There was the sound of running feet. Two Keepers were standing at the spot where Marc had come over the wall.

"I'm sure I heard something," said one.

"Perhaps over there," said the other. He pointed at Marc's hiding place. "Among those bushes?"

Marc was scared. The Keepers were walking towards his hiding place!

Chapter 3
Sasha

Then Marc felt a sharp tug on the hood of his cloak.

"I'm Sasha. Follow me," a voice said in his ear.

He looked round and saw a girl with short dark hair, just behind him. She wore the purple cloak of the Chosen Ones.

"Hurry!" she hissed.

Then she ran off through the trees. Marc ran after her. Soon they came to the first houses of the City. They all had high wooden fences round them. Sasha went up to one of the fences and put her hand on it. Part of the fence slid to one side.

She winked at Marc.

"In you go," she said.

Sasha slipped through after him and closed the fence up again.

"That should hold them up for a bit," she said.

She led Marc down a path and out onto the streets. Marc had never been inside the Fortress before. He had never seen anywhere so wonderful. The gardens were full of flowers.

The walls of the houses and offices looked pink in the light from the setting suns.

They walked on for a little bit, and then the girl turned to Marc.

"Have you got it with you?" she asked.

"What?" said Marc.

"The message capsule with the SOS?"

Marc felt sick. His hands were damp with fear.

"I don't know what you are talking about," he said.

"We don't have time to play silly games," Sasha said. "Have you got the SOS message from the Outsiders?"

Marc said nothing.

Sasha smiled. "I know what you are thinking. *How do I know that I can trust her?*"

"Well?" said Marc. "How *do* I know I can trust you?"

She grinned at him. "You can't. Not for sure. But ..." She looked at Marc for a long moment. "I will show you that I trust you. I will tell you who I am."

"You've told me who you are. You said that your name was Sasha," said Marc.

"Yes, I am Sasha ... but ... I am Alex too."

"Alex!" cried Marc. "Alex, the spy! The one inside the Fortress who tells the Outsiders what is going on?"

"Yes," said Sasha. "Everyone inside the Fortress calls me Sasha. But I use the name Alex when I send news to the Outsiders."

Marc waited, still not sure. "I only know you as Sasha," he said. "I still don't know if I can trust you."

"Look," said Sasha. "At this moment there's nothing else you can do. You *have* to trust me."

Chapter 4
Inside the Fortress

"Yes," Marc said after a pause. "I *have* got the message capsule."

"Then we must hurry," said Sasha. "Soon the streets will not be safe. Everyone must be back in their own homes just one hour after the suns set. Anyone still in the streets after that time is arrested."

She walked off down the street. Marc
waited a moment. Then he went after her.
He pulled Sasha into a doorway where they
would not be seen.

"This is not the way to the Main Square," said Marc.

"We are not going there," said Sasha.

"But Con said I must go to the Main Square," said Marc.

"No," said Sasha. "We are going to the Radio Control Station. We can put the message capsule in the transmitter there and send it out to the Starship."

"How can we get into the Radio Control Station?" said Marc.

"I can get us both inside," said Sasha. "As long as we get there before dark."

Marc shook his head. He did not want to follow Sasha. He had to meet Con in the Main Square. He must go there first.

"How do I get to the Main Square?" he asked Sasha.

"That way," Sasha told him. "But ..."

Marc was about to step out from the doorway, when Sasha dragged him back. Some Keepers went past.

"There are more of them about tonight," said Sasha. Marc could see she was scared. "We must hurry to the Radio Control Station."

"No," said Marc. "I'm not going anywhere until I've seen Con."

Sasha turned then and looked at him.

"Don't you know?" she asked. "Con has been arrested."

Chapter 5
Con

"No!" cried Marc. He felt as if he had been hit.

"I'm sorry," said Sasha. "I thought you knew."

"When ..." asked Marc.

"This afternoon," said Sasha.

"I've been hiding in the bushes all day," said Marc. "No way could I have known that Con had been arrested."

"Everyone in the Fortress is talking about it," said Sasha. "That is why I came to find you at the wall. Jared will force Con to tell him the truth." She took Marc's arm. "You see now why we must hurry. Soon Con will tell Jared everything."

"He'll never talk," said Marc.

Sasha looked at Marc. "Those who are taken by Jared the Keeper," she said, "all talk in the end."

"We have to rescue him," Marc said.

Sasha shook her head. "It is no good. Even I cannot get past the prison guards."

"But we must try," said Marc.

Marc felt sick. Con was their leader.
This was all his plan. He'd made them think
that they could get a message to the
Starship as it passed. If he had been
arrested, then there was no hope.

"I'm going to try to free him," said Marc.

"And how will you do that?" said Sasha. "He's in the Prison. Only Keepers can go in and out, and they are checked at six different gates."

"I don't care," said Marc. "He has done so much for us. Now, I must help him."

"You don't understand, do you?" Sasha said.

"No," yelled Marc. "It is YOU who do not understand. You are one of the Chosen Ones. You have a fine life. We work in the mines all day. You are never hungry or cold. Look at your warm clothes ... and then look at what I wear."

He showed her the dirty, torn clothes he was wearing.

"There's no time to argue," Sasha told him. "We must go to the Radio Control Station now."

"You're right," said Marc. "I won't argue with you. "I'm going to the Prison now."

Sasha blocked his way.

"Listen to me," she said. "You have the message capsule. It MUST be sent out tonight. If you go to the Prison you, too, may be taken. Think about it. What would Con want you to do?"

Chapter 6
A Disagreement

"He would want me to help him escape," Marc said at once. "He would want to be free."

"I, too, would like to be free," said Sasha.

Marc laughed. "You *are* free. You live in the Fortress."

"Yes," said Sasha. "I live in the Fortress. But I am not free. We are all scared here.

29

There are spies all around us. We cannot say what we want, or go where we please. We trust no-one. They choose the films we see and the books we read."

"What!" said Marc. "You would rather live on the Outside where nothing grows, no grass, no trees?"

"Perhaps," said Sasha. "They say that it was beautiful a long time ago, before the Keepers destroyed it all. And it could be that way again if the Outsiders and the people in the Fortress work together."

"But first we must get rid of the Keepers," said Marc.

"Yes, we must," said Sasha.

Chapter 7
Jared the Keeper

Marc nodded his head. "You're right," he said.

 Sasha took his arm. "This way," she said.

Marc kept his hood up as he and Sasha walked through the side streets.

No-one stopped them. Everyone was hurrying to get back home before dark. They came to the Radio Control Station.

"Here we are," said Sasha. "We mustn't go in together. The gate will open when you put this card in the slot."

She gave Marc a thin plastic card.

"Where did you get this?" asked Marc.

Sasha smiled. "There are others in the Fortress who think as I do. When we're inside, we'll go to the basement. Then, we can creep along the air ducts to reach the room where they send out the electronic messages."

Ten minutes later, Sasha and Marc were creeping along the air ducts. The passages were filthy and full of twists and turns. Sasha went first, as quick as a cat. At last she stopped beside a metal grid.

She looked through the slats of the grid.

"Here," she said softly. "My spies say that just after the suns set, the man in charge has a break for 10 minutes. We'll wait."

This is worse than hiding in the bushes all day, thought Marc. They didn't dare to move. They listened and waited.

Then Sasha put her hand on his arm. "He's gone out of the room," she said. She took a sharp tool from under her cloak and with Marc's help opened the metal grid. They got down into the room.

"The transmitter is just there," said Sasha, pointing to a platform.

"Let's send the message now," said Marc.

He got out the capsule from his jerkin.

Sasha took it from him.

"So small, yet so important," he said.

Then Marc heard a noise outside the door. He grabbed Sasha's arm.

"Listen," he said.

There were footsteps in the passage.

"Someone's coming," said Marc.

Sasha peeped through the glass panel at the top of the door.

She turned to Marc. She was shaking.

"We're lost," she cried. "We're lost. It is Jared the Keeper."

She shrank behind the door as it was flung open. A tall man stood in the doorway.

"Hello, Marc," he said. "We meet again."

"Con!" Marc shouted out. "You're free! How did you escape?"

Then Marc saw that Con was not smiling. His face was grim.

"It was very easy to escape," said Con. "I have my own key. The Prison belongs to me."

"What do you mean?" asked Marc.

And then he worked out what Sasha had said before she hid behind the door. "We are lost ... It is Jared ..."

"Let me tell you who I am, boy," said the man. "I am Con ... to you. But ... I am also Jared the Keeper."

Chapter 8
Betrayed

Marc fell back.

"Is this a trick?" he gasped.

"Yes, it is," said Jared. "And it's a very good one. Let me explain it to you, boy." He came closer to Marc. "The Outsiders know that a Starship from Earth comes close to our planet every 20 years. And ..." Jared spoke very slowly, "... we, the Keepers, *know* that they know this. Every 20 years we *expect* the Outsiders to try to send an SOS to the Starship from Earth."

Jared sneered at Marc. "So this time, I didn't wait for the Outsiders to try to get a message out. I decided to plan it myself. Then I would know exactly what you were all up to."

"You have betrayed us!" cried Marc.

"You could say that," said Jared. "But I think that I have saved you too. In the past, lots of Outsiders died when they attacked the Fortress. My plan has stopped all that."

"Why did you let me get this far?" Marc sobbed. He was in tears.

"I did not mean to let you get to the Radio Control Station," said Jared. "You should have been arrested at the gate, or in the Main Square. When no-one had seen you there, I came here to check, just in case you'd got inside the transmitting room."

"Why didn't you stick to the plan to meet me in the Main Square?" said Marc. "Why did you make everyone think that Con was in Prison?"

"I did not want people to see me with you in the Square. Many in the Fortress know what Jared looks like. No-one must find out that Con and Jared are the same person. I want to be able to go back to the Outsiders as Con. I will tell them that the plan failed. And then," Jared gave a wicked smile, "I will help them make a new plan for the next time the Starship comes."

"You won't always win," Marc told him. "Next time someone smarter will take my place."

"Don't be too hard on yourself, boy," said Jared. "You did very well to get this far. I thought that you would go to the Main Square, or, if you heard Con was in Prison, you would go there to rescue him."

"I planned to go," said Marc, "but ..."

He didn't say any more. Sasha! It had been Sasha who had stopped him trying to rescue Con. It was Sasha who'd helped him get here. Where was she? What was she doing?

Jared went on. "I will deal with you, and then I must find out who this spy Alex is. But first, give me the message capsule."

"I expect that's a fake too," said Marc.

"No," said Jared. "You Outsiders know about electronics. You would have seen at

once that the message was a fake. The
message capsule itself is real."

Marc held his breath. Sasha had the
message capsule! And Jared had not seen
her. He did not know who the spy called
Alex was. He did not know about Sasha!
There was still hope!

"Give me the message capsule," said
Jared.

"What?" said Marc.

Marc now wanted to delay Jared. He
could see Sasha behind Jared's back,
creeping along the wall to the transmitter.
She had the message capsule in her hand.
She was going to try to send the message!
Marc saw that he had to gain her a bit
more time.

Marc looked back to Jared. "But ... but I
still don't understand," he said.

"There is nothing more for you to understand, boy," said Jared angrily. "Give me the message capsule."

"No," said Marc.

"This is stupid," said Jared. "You have nothing to gain by keeping it." He pulled his laser gun from his belt. "Give it to me."

"I'd rather die," said Marc.

"Then die you will," said Jared, and he lifted his arm to shoot.

Chapter 9
Starship Rescue

"You'll die with me," said Marc.

"What do you mean?" asked Jared.

"You cannot fire a laser gun in here," said Marc. "This room's too small."

Jared shook his head.

"You're wrong," he said.

Marc was frantic. He must keep Jared talking.

He spoke fast. "In such a small space the blast would be huge. It would kill you too."

"No, you're wrong," said Jared. "And you know it." He stared at Marc for a moment, looking puzzled. "You are only playing for time. Why?"

Marc stared back.

"Why?" Jared asked again. "Why are you trying to delay me?"

Marc said nothing.

Jared stepped across the room and grabbed Marc's arm.

"Give me the message capsule. Now!"

Marc tried to escape, but Jared's grip was firm. As he tried to get free, Marc saw Sasha race to the transmitter platform.

But as Marc saw her ... so did Jared.

"Ah!" he yelled. "Now I see what this is all about! There's another traitor here!"

He raised his laser gun and took aim.

"Stand back from the transmitter!" he yelled at Sasha. "Stand back or I fire!"

Sasha turned. She had opened the sending slot at the front of the transmitter.

All she had to do now was to drop the message capsule inside, close the slot and press the start button. It would only take about three seconds. But Sasha realised that it was three seconds she did not have.

Her hand that held the capsule fell to her side.

Jared smiled.

"Well done," he said.

Marc's body went limp. It was all over. The Outsiders had lost again. Jared let go his grip on Marc's arm and he slumped to the floor.

And then Marc saw Sasha's arm move. She had been bluffing so that Jared would not shoot at her. She was going to do it!

"Stupid girl," Jared shouted at her.

Jared fired his laser gun, but as he did so, Marc jumped up and knocked it out of his hand.

Sasha yelled as she was hit. She clutched her arm. The capsule fell from her hand and rolled across the floor.

As Jared bent down to pick up his laser gun, Marc kicked it away. Jared went after it, and Marc ran to help Sasha. She had picked up the capsule.

"Don't think about me," she sobbed. "Send out the message."

Marc grabbed the capsule from her and put it in the sending slot.

"Press that button and I will kill you."
Jared came towards him.

Marc looked at him. "Too late," he said,
and he pressed the button.

There was silence in the room. Jared's
face was hard and angry.

"You are too late, Jared," Marc said
again. "Even if you had fired your gun, the
message would still have gone. We both
know that it only takes a micro-second to
transmit."

Jared gave a twisted smile. "So in the
end, you were the smart one, boy." He
backed away from Sasha and Marc. "Now, I
think I'll go," he said.

"Please stay where you are," said
someone right behind him.

Four officers wearing Starfleet Security uniform had just come into the room.

One of them took off her helmet.

"I am Captain Mary Rand, Head of Security on Starship 9. We have come down to answer a distress call. Who can tell me what is going on here?"

Marc looked around. Two of the team had gone to take Jared's gun from him. The other officer was looking after the laser burn on Sasha's arm.

"I can try," said Marc.

Chapter 10
Mission Over?

"This is the life for me," Marc told Sasha later.

She was resting in hospital while her burn healed. Marc stood beside her bed eating an orange.

On a table in front of him was a bowl with different kinds of fruit. Every so often

Marc picked one up, and had a good look at it.

"I've never seen so much fruit," he said.

Sasha smiled.

"Please stop talking about food for one moment and tell me what is going on in the Fortress," she said.

"Starfleet Security have taken over," said Marc. "They are setting up a new Council to rule our planet. The Outsiders and the people in the Fortress will work together. The Keepers have been arrested."

"And where is Jared now?" said Sasha.

"He has been taken to the Starship," said Marc. "They say that he will be sent back to Earth to be tried and punished."

"So our work is done," Sasha said.

Marc bit into an apple. He grinned at Sasha.

"I think it may have just begun," he said.

Great reads – no problem!

Barrington Stoke books are:

Great stories – funny, scary or exciting – all by the best writers around!

No hassle – fast reads with no boring bits, and a brilliant story that you can't put down.

Short – the perfect size for a fast, fun read.

We use our own font and paper to make it easier to read our books. And we ask readers like you to check every book before it's published.

That way, we know for sure that every Barrington Stoke book is a great read for everyone.

Check out www.barringtonstoke.co.uk for more info about Barrington Stoke and our books!

If you loved this story, why don't you read ...

The Best in the World

by Chris Powling

Have you ever wanted to push yourself to the limit? Lucas and Jeb are ready to do the "Triple" and become the best trapeze artists in the world. But will they risk their lives to follow a dream?

4u2read.ok!

You can order this book directly from our website
www.barringtonstoke.co.uk

If you loved this story, why don't you read ...

Dead Cool

by Peter Clover

Do you like wacky stories? When Sammy's parents bring him home a parrot in an old, old cage, he gets more than he ever expected. Soon there are pirate ghosts all over the house, but only Sammy can see them! Can he help them to escape from their awful old captain Red Beard the Really Rotten?

4u2read.ok!

If you loved this story, why don't you read ...

Ghost for Sale

by Terry Deary

Would you like to see a ghost? Mr and Mrs Rundle buy a wardrobe with a ghost in it so that people will come to their inn, but the result is not quite what they expect.

4u2read.ok!

You can order this book directly from our website
www.barringtonstoke.co.uk

If you loved this story, why don't you read ...

Looking for Billie

by Rosie Rushton

How far would you go to find your real mum? Billie Gold heard a woman on a train say that she's "looking for Billie". She must be her mum! But how will Billie ever get to talk to her when everything keeps getting in the way?

4u2read.ok!

You can order this book directly from our website
www.barringtonstoke.co.uk

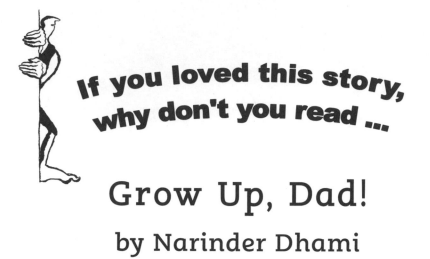

If you loved this story, why don't you read ...

Grow Up, Dad!

by Narinder Dhami

Do you ever feel as if your dad doesn't understand you? Robbie does. His dad just doesn't know how he feels. Until one day, with a bit of magic, things change forever ...

4u2read.ok!

You can order this book directly from our website
www.barringtonstoke.co.uk